Sam and the TIGERS

A New Telling of LITTLE BLACK SAMBO

by JULIUS LESTER / pictures by JERRY PINKNEY

Dial Books for Young Readers New York

Several years ago while browsing through the library of the Charles Blockson Afro-American Collection at Temple University, my wife, Gloria Jean, and I found a number of editions of *Little Black Sambo*. I was amazed at the variety of the artwork in those books; at that time I knew only of the version I had owned as a child. I remembered it well; it is the only picture book depicting a black child that I can recall seeing. I started thinking seriously about a new version and obtained a facsimile of Bannerman's original book, then contacted Helen Mullen of the Free Library of Philadelphia for aid with research. I discovered there were as many as fifty versions of the book, and I struggled to find my own approach to right the wrongs of the original and several subsequent versions.

Meanwhile Julius Lester, who was researching the story, heard of my interest through the Internet. He contacted me about collaborating, as we had for *John Henry,* and we quickly gained the support of Phyllis Fogelman, our editor at Dial. As I began the sketches for Julius's extraordinary text, I was able to find more versions of *Sambo.* Lois Sarkisian of Every Picture Tells a Story, a gallery in Los Angeles, showed me a number of copies. Fran Emery of Fran's Bookhouse in Philadelphia sent me *Sambo Sahib,* a history of Bannerman and her book. Then Phyllis and I went to a rare-book dealer to view many more editions, including a die-cut book and a pop-up.

All this was liberating for me. My thanks go to all who assisted my research, thus freeing me to find my own interpretation of the young black child who could outwit tigers.

J.P.

Published by Dial Books for Young Readers
A Division of Penguin Books USA Inc.
375 Hudson Street
New York, New York 10014
Text copyright © 1996 by Julius Lester
Pictures copyright © 1996 by Jerry Pinkney
All rights reserved
Typography by Jane Byers Bierhorst
Printed in the U.S.A.
First Edition
10 9 8 7 6 5 4 3 2 1

Library of Congress Cataloging in Publication Data

Lester, Julius.
Sam and the tigers / by Julius Lester
pictures by Jerry Pinkney.—1st ed.
p. cm.
Summary / Relates what happens when a little
boy named Sam matches wits with several tigers
that want to eat him (a new telling of *Little Black Sambo*).
ISBN 0-8037-2028-9 (trade).—ISBN 0-8037-2029-7 (lib. bdg.)
[1. Tigers—Fiction. 2. Humorous stories.]
I. Pinkney, Jerry, ill. II. Bannerman, Helen, 1862–1946.
Story of Little Black Sambo. 1996. III. Title.
PZ7.L5629Sam 1996 [E]—dc20 95-43080 CIP AC

*The full-color artwork was
prepared using pencil and watercolor.*

To the Internet
and those on rec.arts.books.children and Child Lit

J.L.

For my grandchildren
and those who share stories generation to generation

J.P.

Once upon a time there was a place called Sam-sam-sa-mara, where the animals and the people lived and worked together like they didn't know they weren't supposed to.

There was a little boy in Sam-sam-sa-mara named Sam. Sam's mama was also named Sam. So was Sam's daddy. In fact, all the people in Sam-sam-sa-mara were named Sam. But nobody ever got confused about which Sam was which, and that's why nobody was named Joleen or Natisha or Willie.

One day Sam and Sam and Sam went to the marketplace to get some new clothes for school. The first place they went was Mr. Elephant's Elegant Habiliments. (Mr. Elephant liked words as big as him that nobody could say.)

Sam's mother picked out a nice brown jacket and white shirt. "That will look very handsome on you."

Sam shook his head. "Uh-uh. That ain't me," he declared.

"Don't you be talking back to your mama like that," Sam said.

"I'm a big boy now. I want to pick out my own clothes!"

Sam looked at Sam. Sam shrugged. Sam shrugged back. Sam nodded. Sam nodded back. Sam and Sam looked at Sam and nodded together. Sam grinned.

Sam looked through the clothes like he was searching for truth. Finally he shouted, "That's what I want!" He held up a coat as red as a happy heart.

Sam started to protest. "You can't wear something like–"

Sam stopped Sam. "He's a big boy now. We've got to let him make his own decisions."

Sam paid Mr. Elephant for the red coat, and off they went to Monkey's Magnificent Attire to look for pants.

Sam looked until he found a pair of pants as purple as a love that would last forever.

Sam shook her head, sighed, and paid Mrs. Monkey for the pants. Off they went to The Feline's Finest Finery to look for a shirt.

Sam picked out one as yellow as tomorrow. "Yes!" he shouted.

Sam shuddered, paid Miss Cat for the yellow shirt, and off they went to Mr. Giraffe's Genuine Stupendous Footwear Emporium.

Sam found a pair of silver shoes shining like promises that are always kept.

Sam paid Mr. Giraffe and closed her pocketbook. "That's it!" she declared. "We've got all your clothes. Let's go home."

Sam shook his head. "I ain't through yet."

"You got a new coat, a new pair of pants, a new shirt, and new shoes. What else do you need?"

"I'm not sure, but I'll know it when I see it."

Sam and Sam followed Sam through the marketplace. He looked and looked and looked until finally, "Yes!" He pointed to an umbrella as green as a satisfied mind. Sam paid Brer Rabbit and then they went home.

The next morning was the first day of school. Sam put on his new clothes and looked at himself in the mirror. "Ain't I fine!" he declared.

Sam went downstairs to breakfast, his new clothes shining brighter than Mr. Sun when he comes back from his winter vacation. Sam and Sam had to put on sunglasses to protect their eyes from all the colors Sam was wearing.

"You better be careful," Sam said. "You might put Mr. Sun out of business."

"If I knew how to sit in the sky without a chair, I would."

Sam and Sam kissed Sam good-bye, and he headed off for school.

Sam had not gone very far before he saw a Tiger coming toward him. The Tiger stopped and looked at Sam. Sam stopped and looked at the Tiger.

"Sam, I'm going to eat you up," said the Tiger.

Sam shook his head. "I don't like that idea. Why don't you take my red coat instead?"

The Tiger looked at the coat. "Nice coat. It's a deal, Sam."

Sam took off his coat and gave it to the Tiger. The Tiger put it on. "Ain't I fine!" said the Tiger.

"Yes, you are," agreed Sam.

The Tiger went on his way. Sam went on his.

Before long here come another Tiger. The Tiger stopped and looked at Sam. Sam stopped and looked at the Tiger.

"Sam, I'm going to eat you up."

Sam shook his head. "I don't like that idea. Why don't you take my pretty yellow shirt?"

The Tiger looked at the shirt. "Nice shirt, Sam. It's a deal."

Sam took off his shirt and gave it to the Tiger. The Tiger put it on. "Ain't I fine!" he exclaimed.

"You are indeed," Sam agreed.

The Tiger went on his way. Sam went on his.

Sam had an idea of what kind of day it was going to be, and when he saw the next Tiger coming, he took off his shoes. "Here you go," Sam said, holding out the shoes.

"Good deal for you. Bad deal for me. I've got four feet. You only got two shoes."

"Feet!" Sam exclaimed. "These are ear-shoes!"

The Tiger put them on. "Ain't I fine!" he declared.

"You are indeed," Sam agreed.

The Tiger went on his way.

Sam didn't see any point in moving, and sure enough, along came another Tiger.

"Here," Sam said, offering the Tiger his green umbrella.

"Tigers don't need umbrellas!" he declared. "I'm going to eat you, Sam."

"If you do, it'll send your cholesterol way up," Sam began. "Don't you understand? You could be the first Tiger smart enough to carry an umbrella."

"What would I carry it with? I need my feet for walking."

"Use your tail."

Tiger wrapped his tail around the umbrella and held it over his head. "Ain't I fine!" he exclaimed.

"Indeed you are!" agreed Sam.

The Tiger went on his way.

Sam went on his, hoping he wouldn't see another Tiger. All he had left was his purple pants. Before his hope had time to take a good look around, here come another Tiger.

"You know the routine," said the Tiger.

Sam nodded and took off his pants. "Take 'em."

The Tiger put them on. "Ain't I fine!" he declared.

"I could care less," Sam pouted. "Look at me." Sam stood there in his underwear.

"Bad day, Sam," Tiger said, and went on his way.

Sam started crying. He cried and he cried and he cried. Sam might still be crying if he hadn't heard a loud and very scary noise.

"Grrrrr!"

"What was that?"

"GRRRRRR!"

"It's the Tigers! They don't like my clothes and they've come back to eat me!"

Sam hid behind a big tree and peeped out. In a clearing he saw the Tigers strutting around in a circle.

"I'm the finest," growled the Tiger in the red coat.

"No way, Insect Breath! I'm the finest!" said the Tiger in the yellow shirt.

"Uh-uh!" declared the Tiger with the silver shoes on his ears. "I'm finer than you two losers."

"No way!" proclaimed the Tiger carrying the green umbrella in his tail. "I'm the finest."

"You make me laugh," snorted the Tiger wearing the purple pants. "I am the finest Tiger that ever was, ever is, and ever will be."

The Tigers were so angry, they were ready to fight. Tiger took off his red coat. Tiger took off his yellow shirt. Tiger took off his purple pants. Tiger took off his silver shoes. Tiger let the green umbrella drop from his tail onto the ground.

They snarled and growled and snapped at each other until, suddenly, they were rolling and wrestling and wrestling and rolling on the ground. They wrestled and rolled and snarled and snapped right up to the tree where Sam was hiding.

Sam ran to the clearing and peered out from behind the green
umbrella to see what was going on. The Tigers were running around
the tree, each one holding the tail of another Tiger in his jaws, each
trying to catch the other.

"Hey! Tigers!" Sam called. "Don't you want your clothes anymore?"

"Grrrrrrrrrrr!" The Tigers ran faster.

"If you do, you better say something. If you don't, I'm going to take
them!"

"GRRRRRRRRRRRRRRRR!" The Tigers ran faster and faster.

Sam put on his yellow shirt and then his purple pants, his red
coat, and finally his silver-shiny shoes. "Ain't I fine!" he announced to
the Tigers, holding the green umbrella up like a victory flag.

The Tigers saw Sam wearing their clothes and that made them very, very angry. But they wouldn't let go of each other's tails. Instead they ran faster and faster until all Sam could see was a blur!

Faster and faster and faster and faster the Tigers ran until–they
melted into a pool of butter as golden as a dream come true.

A few minutes later Sam and Sam came back with Miss Cat, Mr. Elephant, Brer Rabbit, Mrs. Monkey, Mr. Giraffe, Brer Fox, and Brer Wolf. They were talking about the happenings in the community. Seems like five Tigers had disappeared that morning and nobody could find them. Sam smiled but didn't say a word.

Everybody sat down to eat, exclaiming that these were the best pancakes ever made on the front side of the earth!

Sam ate twenty-seven, Sam ate fifty-five, but *Sam* ate a hundred and sixty-nine.

Wearing all them colors can really make a boy hungry.

In 1899 a book called *Little Black Sambo* was published. There are two versions of how it came to be. Helen Bannerman, a Scot, was married to a doctor in the British military and living in India. In one version, she writes and illustrates the story for her two daughters attending school back in Scotland. The other has the family living in India and Bannerman writing it on a train when she was separated from her daughters. Whatever the specifics, the story was written as entertainment by a mother for her daughters. Despite its black characters, the story is not set in Africa. Nor is it set in India, despite the tigers. The setting is fanciful and was never meant to be taken literally.

It would be unfair to say Bannerman had a racist intent in creating *Little Black Sambo*. However, it was published during the era of social Darwinism, which argued that societies, like nature, were ruled by the doctrine of the "survival of the fittest." History had "proven" that whites were the most "fit" and people of black African descent the least. Intentionally or not, *Little Black Sambo* reinforced the idea of white superiority through illustrations exaggerating African physiognomy and a name, Sambo, that had been used negatively for blacks since the early seventeenth century.

Yet the story transcended its stereotypes. For almost a century, children have enjoyed it. Jerry Pinkney and I read the story as children and recognized that Sambo was a black hero, but his name and how he was depicted took away his heroic status.

A new telling required reconceptualization. How to retain the fun without the historical baggage? I played with the syllable Sam until one morning "Sam-sam-sa-mara" came out of my mouth. In the same moment I thought, Name all the people Sam! Another problem was Bannerman's language, a model of simplicity I could not imitate. More natural for me was the southern black storytelling voice I employed in the retelling of the Uncle Remus stories, which Jerry Pinkney also illustrated. The final problem was visual. Despite their racism, Jerry saw a mythical quality in Bannerman's illustrations and sought to parallel it.

The biggest challenge for both of us was history. Many whites had loved *Little Black Sambo* as children and were afraid their love of it made them racists now. That is not so. Many blacks, angered and shamed, resolved that it be thrown in the garbage. For many years so had I.

Yet what other story had I read at age seven and remembered for fifty years? There was obviously an abiding truth in the story, despite itself. I think it is the truth of the imagination, that incredible realm where animals and people live together like they don't know any better, and children eat pancakes cooked in the butter of melted tigers, and parents never say, "Don't eat so many."

J.L.

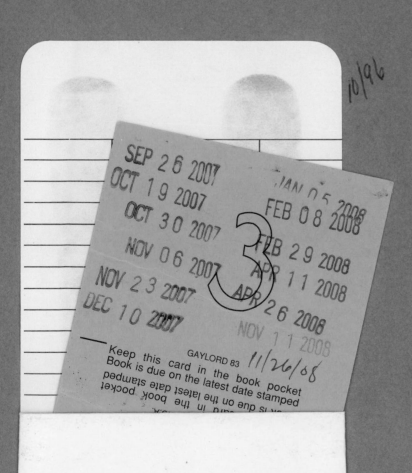